SHERLOCK SAM and the GHOSTLY MOANS in FORT CANNING

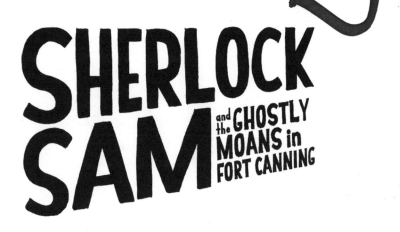

SHER
SAM

By
A.J.
LOW

Andrews McMeel
Publishing®

a division of Andrews McMeel Universal

Epigram Books Pte. Ltd.
1008 Toa Payoh North #03-08 Singapore 318996
Tel: +65 6292 4456 / Fax: +65 6292 4414
enquiry@epigrambooks.sg / www.epigrambooks.sg

Andrews McMeel Publishing
a division of Andrews McMeel Universal
1130 Walnut Street, Kansas City, Missouri 64106

www.andrewsmcmeel.com

16 17 18 19 20 SDB 10 9 8 7 6 5 4 3 2 1

ISBN: 978-1-4494-7788-2

Library of Congress Number: 2015959868

Made by:
Shenzhen Donnelley Printing Company Ltd.
Address and location of manufacturer:
No. 47, Wuhe Nan Road, Bantian Ind. Zone,
Shenzhen China, 518129
1st Printing—5/9/16

FOR THE MUNCHKIN GANG:
Boon, Siva, Lemon, The Meihan, and Highlander

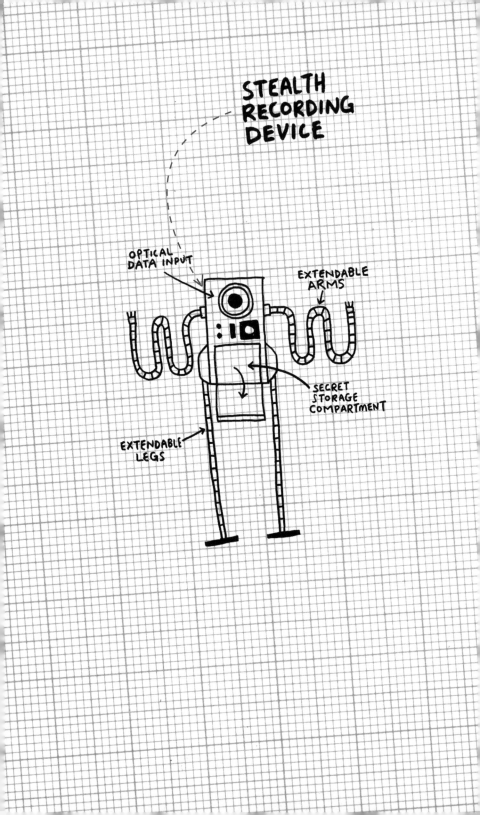

CHAPTER ONE

"Hold still, Watson!" I said.

"I-have-been-holding-still-for-thirty-two-minutes," Watson replied.

"Then just hold still for one . . . more . . . minute," I grumbled, giving the screwdriver one final twist. "There, it's done!"

I stood back to admire my handiwork. Other than the small panel that was open on the right side of Watson's head, he didn't look any different. But he was now more powerful than ever! MUAHAHAHA!

"Why-are-you-laughing-strangely?" Watson asked.

I closed the panel with a sharp click.

"Let's test it out, Watson," I said. "On my mark, start!"

Watson remained silent.

"Watson? Did you hear me? I said 'start,'" I said, and waited for him to respond.

Watson continued to remain silent.

"Is it not working correctly? Impossible!" I said, moving toward my robot.

"Let's test it out, Watson. On my mark, start!" I said in reply.

Wait a minute, was that me?

"Watson? Did you hear me? I said 'start,'" I continued.

Was my voice really that squeaky? But more important, it worked! The new recording device I had installed in Watson worked!

"Isn't this awesome, Watson? Now you will be able to record all my case notes, no matter where we are!" I said.

"Indeed. What-could-be-more-awesome-than-recording-your-case-notes?" Watson replied.

"Okay, let's start with the Case of the Missing Hamster," I replied, glaring at my robot. "He was brown with white patches. At his young age, he was already a proficient escape artist. They called him Benjamin. Benjamin the hamster—"

"Boys! Dinner!" Dad called from the living room.

"Dinner! Come on, Watson!" I said, already halfway out of my bedroom. "Coming, Dad!"

Dad, Mom, and Wendy were seated at the dining table by the time Watson and I arrived. Mom had made her famous spaghetti bolognese! Her sauce has just the right mix of minced beef, carrots, and celery—a delicious savory perfection! Watson had his own plate of used batteries, which he consumes as his power source. His batteries were AA and cold.

"May I have extra cheese, please?" I asked politely.

"You're so chubby already, and you still want more cheese," Wendy said.

I glared at my sister. Wendy is tall and skinny, and only a year older than me. Maybe I will have a growth spurt when I turn eleven. Anyway, great detectives come in all shapes and sizes, and that is what I want to be: a great detective like Sherlock Holmes or Batman!

"It's all right. Sam is a growing boy," Dad replied, handing me the bowl of grated cheese.

"Only one more spoonful, Samuel," Mom warned. She had a look on her face that meant she wasn't going to repeat herself.

"Yes, Mom," I said. I made sure it was a heaping spoonful. Dad grinned at me. Like me, he had been a chubby kid when he was ten, but now he is tall and skinny! I have genetics on my side! I read about this in *The Stuff of Life*, a comic on genes and DNA that Dad bought for me. He also let me read *Science of the X-Men*, which is also about genetics, but not as relevant to my situation.

"What time is your field trip tomorrow morning?" Mom asked.

"Egg-ay-em," I mumbled, my mouth full of pasta.

"Egg-ay-em," Watson repeated.

Everyone turned to look at Watson.

"What was that?!" Wendy asked, her eyes wide.

"Oh. I've just installed a recording program in Watson," I replied, twirling spaghetti around my fork.

"That's interesting," Dad said, nodding approvingly.

"No eavesdropping," Mom said, shaking her head disapprovingly.

"Can Watson help me with my Chinese presentation for school?" Wendy asked.

"No, he may not," Mom replied. "Anyway, both of you have to leave at eight a.m. tomorrow, is that right? And I'm supposed to drop you off at Fort Canning Park?"

"Yes, Mom. All the Upper Primary kids are going to the Battle Box!" I said.

"That's so fun! When I was in school, the only outing we had was to the shiitake mushroom farm at Lim Chu Kang," Dad said. "There are only so many photographs you can take of mushrooms before feeling bored. Those fungi are no fun guys."

"There's a spice garden at Fort Canning, I think," Mom said.

"Do they have mushrooms there?" Dad asked.

"A-mushroom-is-not-a-spice," Watson replied.

"But what is the Battle Box?" Mom asked, smiling fondly at Dad. He is a genius engineer, but often gets his vegetables and fruits mixed up. And, apparently, also his fungi.

"The Battle Box was an underground bunker the British Malaya High Command used as its headquarters during the Second World War. Now it's been converted into a historical attraction," Dad replied. See? Smart!

"Apparently they use animatronics to re-create historical scenes, Dad! How cool is that?" I said.

"I-am-looking-forward-to-meeting-fellow-robots," Watson said.

"I want to see the sculptures at the sculpture garden," Wendy said.

"Wendy, look after your brother," Mom reminded.

"But Mom! My classmates will be there! I'm supposed to be buddies with a new boy. I can't babysit Cher Lock all day!" Wendy cried.

"SHER-lock!" I retorted.

"SHER-lock!" Watson cried in my voice.

I made a mental note to give Watson a command word so that he would know when to start recording, and when to stop. Otherwise, who knew what he would record!

"Well, keep a lookout for Sam and Watson anyway. I'm sure your new friend would love to meet a robot," Mom replied.

"Fine, but you better behave," Wendy said, wrinkling her nose at me.

"I-always-behave," Watson replied.

"Thanks, Watson," I said. Watson is my loyal sidekick. I knew he would always take my side.

"And-I-will-inform-you-if-Sherlock-misbehaves," Watson continued.

Then again, maybe not.

ooo

CHAPTER TWO

"Why are we stopping here?" I asked. Mom had stopped the car alongside what looked like a million steps leading up a hill.

"What do you mean?" Mom replied.

"Don't you know that force equals mass multiplied by acceleration?" I said, incredulous. "Do you know how much acceleration I'll need to get up these steps?"

"Especially-with-your-mass," Watson said.

"Oh! I was just going to say that, Watson!

High five!" Wendy laughed, attempting to slap my robot's hand with hers. Watson, to my pleasure, did not cooperate.

"I'm going to meet my friends for breakfast, Sam. And I'm already late. Your sister said that I could drop you all off here because it leads straight up to the meeting point," Mom replied.

"Come on, Sam! Let's accelerate!" Wendy grinned at me as she slammed the car door shut.

I sighed heavily as I pulled on my heavy backpack. Mom waved cheerily as she drove off.

"Watson, record my last will and testament. I am leaving all my comics to Dad," I recited, taking my final few steps in life, up the first few steps of the stairway leading up to Fort Canning.

"Dad bought you all your comics. He already owns them," Wendy shouted down, already miles ahead of me.

"That's why . . . I'm leaving . . . them . . . to him!" I gasped.

"Exercise-may-help-you-grow-taller," Watson said.

I was pretty sure that wasn't true, but I needed air more than I needed to give a clever response.

By the time I reached the top of the stairs, I had eaten the sandwich Mom had prepared for my lunch. It was the most sensible thing to do: I had to reduce the mass of my backpack so that I would require less force to climb up the steps. However, I decided to keep my astute scientific insights to myself this time around.

"Hey, Sherlock! Hey, Watson! Hey, Wendy! What took you guys so long? I've been here forever! Almost five minutes!" Jimmy greeted us cheerfully, bouncing in excitement.

I peered closely at Jimmy. Neat hair. Dry school T-shirt. Not a bead of sweat on his

upper lip or brow. My deductive abilities kicked into overdrive.

"You took an escalator!" I yelled.

"Yeah, it's over on the other side!" Jimmy replied, pointing in the opposite direction of where Mom had dropped us off.

"He took an escalator!" I yelled again, this time at Wendy.

"He did?" my sister replied. I didn't need my detective skills to recognize the look of fake innocence on her face.

"Come on, Sherlock! We have to meet up with our class. See you later, Wendy!" Jimmy said, pulling Watson and me by our arms.

"Behave yourself, Cher Lock!" Wendy called out.

"It's SHER-lock!" I shouted back, Jimmy dragging me away.

Wendy was already talking to one of her classmates, a tall Malay boy. From the way Wendy repeatedly leaned forward to listen to him, I concluded that he was rather soft-spoken and very likely shy. This must be the new boy she had mentioned at dinner last night. As class monitor, she had been tasked to be his buddy and guide him around.

Fort Canning Park was very large and green, with many uphill slopes that I was not looking forward to climbing. There were wooden signposts everywhere, pointing to various attractions in the park.

Jimmy and I lined up with our class near the Battle Box ticketing office and waited for our teachers to organize the classes into some form of order. Coincidentally, Wendy and her new classmate lined up right next to us.

"Is that a robot?" the new kid asked, his dark brown eyes wide with amazement.

"My-name-is-Wat-son," Watson said. "Sher-lock-has-forbidden-me-to-speak-of-the-special-abilities-I-do-not-have."

I made a note to explain to Watson exactly

what the word *secret* meant when I told him that his abilities were to be kept a secret.

"Wait, Sherlock and Watson? Like in the novels?" the new kid said. "I love Sir Arthur Conan Doyle."

"He's Samuel Tan Cher Lock actually," Wendy said.

"It's always great to meet another fan of a great author. I'm Sherlock Sam," I said, deftly ignoring my sister and reaching out to shake the new kid's hand.

"You're Sherlock Sam? The student that solves mysteries?" the new kid asked. I hoped he would tell me his name soon so I would not have to keep calling him "the new kid."

"My name is Nazhar," the new kid said. "I just changed schools because my family shifted from Punggol to Bedok. I've been hearing about this super clever Primary Four student with a robot. I didn't realize he was your brother, Wendy."

"Oh? I was sure I'd mentioned him to you," my sister replied, deadpan.

". . . and at night, they say that the souls of the dead come out and haunt the grounds," someone in Wendy's class said. Everyone's attention was captured by the words *souls of the dead* and we fell silent and listened in.

"No way," one of the boys said.

The Eurasian girl who had been speaking carried on, ignoring him. "Lots and lots of people were buried here in the past, plus the people who died here during the war. All of Fort Canning is one giant haunted house!"

"There are no such things as ghosts," I said loudly. I couldn't help myself.

The group of kids that the girl had been talking to turned and glared at me.

"Yes, there are," the girl replied snottily. "I bet there are ghosts in the Battle Box bunker!"

Everyone, even the girl's friends, glanced about warily. Nazhar rubbed his neck uncomfortably, as if something had spooked him from behind. Jimmy looked as pale as a . . . well, as pale as a ghost. If ghosts existed.

"There are really no such things as ghosts. Their existence has never been conclusively proven beyond a reasonable doubt," I replied.

"How would you know?" the girl asked. "You're just in P4. I bet you don't even know what a poltergeist is." She crossed her arms smugly.

"Of course I do. It's a ghost that makes itself known by creating loud noises and moving things about," I said. "But it doesn't exist."

"I bet a poltergeist is going to come and get you later!" the girl said loudly, pointing at Jimmy, who already looked terrified. He grabbed Watson, who, surprisingly, let him cling on.

"Eliza, leave my brother and Jimmy alone," Wendy said, stepping in front of Jimmy and me. Just then the teachers started calling out class names, signaling the students to move into the Battle Box in a calm and orderly manner.

All chaos broke loose.

Wendy's class dashed forward while Eliza muttered something about *kaypoh* P4 kids. While Wendy and Nazhar were being pushed along ahead of us, Nazhar turned back to call out, "See you guys later for lunch!"

"I-hope-someone-remembered-to-bring-my-batteries-for-lunch," Watson said.

Oops.

○ ○ ○

CHAPTER THREE

"That-was-disappointing," Watson said.

"What are you talking about, Watson?" Jimmy said. "It was awesome! Sometimes it was scary though. The animal-tropics looked so real!"

"You-mean-animatronics," Watson corrected.

"That's what I said," Jimmy replied.

"Watson is just disappointed that none of the robots were able to have a conversation with him, Jimmy," I said. "In truth, I am a bit disappointed as well. The animatronics were quite passable facsimiles of human beings, but none were sentient."

"They were faxi-what of what?" Jimmy asked, looking terribly confused.

"He means that while the robots looked like humans, they were just simple machines," Nazhar said, appearing with Wendy.

"Did you enjoy the Battle Box, Nazhar?" I asked.

"I thought it was informative, but my dad's a big World War II history buff so I didn't learn anything new," Nazhar replied.

"That's a cool sketch, Wendy," Jimmy said, peering over her shoulder. Wendy had drawn one of the war scenes from the Battle Box, featuring the British commanders. It looked extremely realistic.

"Wendy's a really talented artist," Nazhar said.

From the sudden flush that spread across her cheeks, I deduced that my sister was either embarrassed or pleased. Most likely both. I think my sister will be a famous artist one day. But I'll only tell her when I'm older. And taller.

"Let's eat!" I said. "I would like to explore the Spice Garden after this. It has information on what spices can be used to make food more delicious."

Our teachers told us that we could spread out on Fort Canning Green for lunch. It was a large grassy area in the middle of the park. Events were held there most weekends, and even in the middle of the day, on a weekday, there were a few people there having picnics.

We sat down to eat our food. Nazhar pulled out homemade *nasi lemak*, which looked and smelled delicious! I could smell the rich fragrance of *pandan* leaf and coconut milk, which his mom must have used to cook the rice! I bet it was extra *lemak*!

Jimmy pulled out fried rice and sausages, which also looked and smelled delicious!

His grandma had even given him an extra fried egg!

Wendy pulled out a tuna sandwich, which didn't look or smell as interesting.

Just then, I suddenly remembered that I had eaten my tuna sandwich to lighten my backpack while climbing up those horrible stairs! All I had left were celery and carrot sticks!

"Oh no!" I gasped.

"What's wrong?" Jimmy asked.

"A ghost must have just touched his face!" Eliza interrupted. She was standing behind me, smirking, with a bunch of her giggling friends.

"Please leave him alone, Eliza," Wendy said. "We just want to eat our lunch quickly."

"You know you are sitting on dead bodies, right? They are going to come and haunt you tonight!" Eliza said.

Jimmy immediately jumped to his feet. "What . . . what does she mean we're sitting on dead bodies?" he stammered.

"This used to be a cemetery, Jimmy," Nazhar said. "They buried lots of people here."

"In fact, the carvings on the walls over there are actually old tombstones!" Eliza said snottily. "I bet there are ghosts all around us now!" Eliza and her friends laughed as they walked away.

Jimmy's eyes bugged out and he clutched his face with horror.

"You mean what she said earlier was true? We're sitting on dead bodies?" Jimmy gasped.

"Well, yes," Nazhar replied.

Jimmy's eyes went wider.

"There-is-still-a-small-cemetery-in-the-corner-by-the-Gothic-Gate-on-the-west," Watson said.

Jimmy's eyes were the biggest I had ever seen them.

"I-I-I-I-" Jimmy stammered.

"It's okay, Jimmy, they're dead. They can't hurt you," Wendy said.

"Did you guys know that during World

War II, the Japanese took over Fort Canning from the British and used it as the base of their military operations till the end of the war?" Nazhar said, trying to distract Jimmy.

I had to admit, I did not know that. I was glad Nazhar and I were friends. I am always eager to learn new things. Even Batman has friends and mentors he learns from!

"And during the Japanese occupation, they used a different currency called *duit pisang*. My dad has two notes," Nazhar continued.

"But this place is all haunted! There are ghosts everywhere!" Jimmy said. That was all he could focus on.

"And when they were alive, I'm sure they were very nice people who wouldn't have hurt you anyway," I said. "Besides, there are no such things as ghosts. You trust me, right, Jimmy?"

Jimmy nodded and settled down after that. Everybody continued eating.

My stomach grumbled.

Wendy sighed. "You can have half of my sandwich, Sam."

I ate it quickly, before she could change her mind. Once in a while, having a big sister was a good thing. This is also something I will tell her when I am older. And taller.

Once we finished our lunch, we rushed over to the Spice Garden, as we only had about twenty minutes before we had to head to the school buses. I wanted to make notes on what spices Mom could use to make her cooking more delicious! Plus, perhaps there would be a vending machine that dispensed snacks or Milo!

We walked past a curry leaf bush (good for curry, especially fish curries!), a black pepper plant (pepper is the most popular spice in the world!), and a lemon—

Wendy burst out laughing, startling Nazhar. "I think you need to eat more lemongrass, Sherlock!"

"I don't understand what you mean,"

I replied, quickly moving away from the lemongrass plant. I had read the same information plaque Wendy had seen, and knew exactly why she was laughing.

"It-says-here-that-lemongrass-is-believed-to-relieve-flatulence," Watson said.

Gee, thanks, Watson.

"What's 'flat-you-lance'?" Jimmy asked.

"It's nothing you need to be bothered about, Jimmy," I said.

Even Nazhar was smiling slightly.

Jimmy continued to look confused and I saw Watson whisper something to him. Suddenly, Jimmy burst out laughing and said, "I love fart jokes!"

"Watson, we will speak of your betrayal at home," I said.

"Guys, we should head back," Nazhar said. "It's almost time to line up."

We were heading back, and as we walked to the top of the hill, past the Archaeological Dig and Exhibition Area, Jimmy suddenly decided that racing would be fun.

"Come on, Watson, I'll race you!" Jimmy said, racing off at full speed.

Watson continued to walk at his usual leisurely pace.

Jimmy, however, turning back to look at Watson, tripped, fell head over heels, and tumbled toward the bushes!

"Jimmy!" I yelled. "Are you all right?!"

Jimmy sat up, looking shocked. He grabbed his head and checked it frantically for injuries. Finding no bumps and nothing wrong at all, Jimmy sprang up, grinning, and waved happily at all of us! His school T-shirt was covered in grass and dirt, but he was fine otherwise. Suddenly, he stopped waving and walked farther into the bushes.

"What is that?" Jimmy asked. He was clearing a path through the bushes and poking at a rusty metal gate. "Do you think this is a shortcut?"

"Oh, wow! It's a sally port! That's strange. Dad told me there was only one sally port left in Fort Canning," Nazhar said. He had run forward earlier when Jimmy had tumbled, and had reached the rusty metal gate before the rest of us.

"What's a sally port?" Wendy asked.

"It's a small hidden doorway leading in and

out of a fort. It allows the people who lived in the fort to escape undetected if enemies attack," Nazhar replied. "We saw one near the Battle Box ticket office just now, but the teachers told us not to go there, remember?"

I was impressed. I realized that in order to become the great detective I wanted to be,

I needed to brush up on my history. Note to self: Remind Dad to buy me some books on Singaporean history.

"Wow! Does that mean that Jimmy has found an undiscovered sally port?" Wendy asked.

"Do you think it'll be named after me?" Jimmy asked, wide-eyed. "A Jimmy port!"

"Maybe, Jimmy," Nazhar replied, smiling. "I wonder where it leads. Sherlock, do you think we should check it out?"

"Curious," I replied. "We definitely should. In fact, the Fort Canning authorities might be interested to learn—"

Suddenly, a strange sound came from within the sally port!

"**OOO**ooo**OOO**ooo. **OOO**ooo**OOO**ooo. **OOO**ooo**OOO**ooo."

Nobody moved. We all stared at the newly discovered sally port . . . and waited.

After what seemed an eternity, Wendy said, "Maybe it was just the wind?"

"**OOOoooOOOooo. OOOoooOOOooo. OOOoooOOOooo,**" the sally port replied. Suddenly, a rock flew out of the sally port!

"Ahhhh! A poultry-guest!" Jimmy shouted as he ran, flapping his arms like a chicken.

We all ran after him, even Watson.

ooo

CHAPTER FOUR

"I didn't know Watson could run," Dad said.

"I-did-not-run," Watson replied.

"Watson ran so fast, he lost a screw," I said, holding up Watson's loose screw. I knew robots couldn't fume, but I was sure I heard Watson's circuits crackle even more furiously than normal.

"So tell me again what you heard?" Dad replied, trying to hide his grin.

"It was a ghostly moan," I replied, "but I didn't have sufficient time to definitively pinpoint exactly where it was coming from. It seemed to be coming from the sally port, but given our heightened state of—"

"Being a chicken?" Wendy said, walking past Dad, Watson, and me in the living room.

"You ran away, too!" I said.

"Only because I had to chase after you, Cher Lock!" Wendy replied.

"Dad, Wendy ran so fast, she lost a shoe," I said, holding up Wendy's lost shoe.

In response, Wendy shut her door very firmly with a loud click.

"So the reason you want me to take you back to Fort Canning tonight is . . . ?" Dad asked.

"There are no such things as ghosts, Dad!" I said. "You've always said! And now we have to prove it! Right, Watson?"

"If-you-do-not-believe-in-ghosts-there-is-no-need-to-prove-it," Watson replied.

Clearly, the loose screw was affecting Watson's ability to process information in a logical manner. "We are going to use science, Dad! Just like Neil deGrasse Tyson, your hero!" I said.

"SCIENCE!" Dad said, standing up with his feet firmly planted apart, one hand braced on his hip, the other hand raised, his index finger pointing up in triumph. Dad always strikes this pose when he says, "SCIENCE!" He is, quite possibly, the best dad ever.

"If SCIENCE is at stake, then let's go!" Dad said.

Mom looked at us oddly as Dad, Watson, and I marched out with large backpacks, but

she quickly went back to her book. "It's a school night, so be back by eleven," she said.

Dad had packed plenty of scientific equipment that could double as ghost-hunting equipment, including an electromagnetic field (EMF) meter, a digital recorder, a digital thermometer, and flashlights. The EMF meter was to check for electromagnetic disturbances, the digital recorder was to check for sounds not in the range of human hearing, the thermometer was to check if the temperature was lower than the surroundings, and the flashlights were because it would be dark. Obviously.

Dad drove Watson and me back to Fort Canning and we all trooped out of the car, intrepid adventurers in the night.

"So, we should first re-create the exact scenario leading up to when you heard the ghostly wail," Dad said, armed with a flashlight and the digital recorder.

"It was more of a ghostly moan than a wail," I replied. It was very important to be precise. We decided to start at the most likely source of the disturbance: the cemetery. I was in charge of the digital thermometer while Watson had the EMF meter.

"Watson, you should take the lead," I said.

"Why-should-I-take-the-lead?" Watson asked.

"Because robots are stealthy, as you're always telling me," I replied triumphantly. "Also, your headlamp is the brightest."

Watson walked ahead of us while Dad and I trailed after, our flashlights slowly moving along the tombstones in the walls, which had names of deceased Europeans carved into them. We checked if any of the tombstones had been disturbed recently. "What are the chances that there could be a zombie infestation?" I asked Dad.

Ghosts were one thing; zombies were another. There were even zombie preparedness websites on the Internet! Dad had made zombie preparedness packs for all of us because, he says, "If you're equipped to deal with a zombie attack, you're equipped to deal with earthquakes, tsunamis, and generally everything else in between!" Mom calls them our emergency packs, but Dad and I call them our Zombie Apocalypse Packs, or ZAP Packs for short. (The term *ZAP Packs* would technically stand for Zombie Apocalypse Packs Packs, but "ZAP Packs" is more fun to say.)

"Slim, I would say. The police would have arrived to break up an illegal gathering of that size by now," Dad replied. "Besides, there has been no increase in patients who have been bitten at the hospital. I checked before we left the house."

Dad was right, of course. The grave sites were undisturbed. No upturned soil. No overturned headstones. No choreographed dancing.

"I see no evidence of any supernatural activity here, Sam," Dad said finally.

"Neither do I, Dad," I replied, pleased.

"How about you, Watson?"

"I-have-found-something-supernatural," Watson said.

"What?!" Dad and I looked around frantically.

"I-am-beyond-natural. Therefore-I-am-supernatural," Watson said.

Dad and I gave Watson a withering look. "Very funny," I mumbled.

We looked around a bit more, but found nothing.

"If we hurry, we could get some *tau huay* and *you char kway* before heading home!" I said brightly. I love the combination of the warm soybean curd and the deep-fried dough sticks. My favorite part is dipping the *you char kway* into the *tau huay* and sucking all the liquid out before crunching down. Yummy!

"Good thinking, son. The famous Rochor Original Beancurd is at Selegie, just a five-minute drive away. I think Mom and Wendy might like some, too," Dad replied.

We walked back up to the newly discovered sally port (or "Jimmy port" as Jimmy had taken to calling it) where we had originally heard the noise. Hotel Fort Canning was nearby, past the Fort Canning Centre.

Dad had called the hotel earlier, pretending to make a reservation, and had taken the opportunity to ask the concierge if there had been any strange reports in the area. For example, had any guests reported hearing ghostly moans at night? The concierge quickly mentioned that Fort Canning was a historical site and that there were many rumors that had never been proven. He followed up with a description of the hotel's lovely buffet breakfast. A devious distraction tactic!

"We should see if Mom and Wendy would like a staycation one weekend," Dad said. "Once your exams are over!"

"That would be—" I began to say.

"**OOOoooOOOooo. OOOoooOOOooo. OOOoooOOOooo.**"

We froze in the exact same spot that we had been in before, right in front of the sally port that Jimmy had discovered.

I heard Dad gulp loudly.

"Nobody move," he whispered. "Was . . . was this the sound you heard earlier?"

I nodded. There are no such things as ghosts, there are no such things as ghosts.

"**OOOoooOOOooo. OOOoooOOOooo. OOOoooOOOooo.**"

At night, with the park almost completely silent, the sally port's strange moans seemed louder than they did in the afternoon! Plus, was it my imagination, or did the moans seem even closer as well?

"It-would-be-wise-for-us-to-make-our-getaway-now," Watson said.

Dad and I were frozen in place.

Watson extended his arms, wrapped one around me and one around Dad, and lifted us over his head. He ran straight to the car, with us screaming all the way.

We never did stop for *tau huay* and *you char kway*.

ooo

CHAPTER FIVE

"ARRRRRRGGGGGGHHHHHHHHHH!!!!!!"
Watson said.

I could have pretended that the sound being played back by Watson was doctored or made up, but I am a boy of fact! The fact was that Dad and I had yelled all the way back to the car. We drove home at a speed nearing the speed of light.

"I think that's enough, Watson. Jimmy gets the idea," I said. We were in the school hall, waiting for assembly to start.

The ARRGGHHING-ing stopped mid-ARGH.

"So what are you saying, Sherlock? That ghosts are real?" Jimmy asked. He seemed distracted, digging in his bag, then in his pockets, frowning.

"There are no such things as ghosts!" I said adamantly.

"Hmm . . . " Jimmy replied. Now I knew for sure that something was wrong. Jimmy was acting far too calm in the face of possible ghosts.

"What's wrong, Jimmy?" I asked.

"I think I left my wallet at home!" Jimmy replied. "I have no money for lunch!"

"That's terrible! What are you going to do?" I said. I couldn't imagine having nothing to eat for lunch!

"Can I borrow two dollars from you? I'll pay you back tomorrow immediately!" Jimmy said.

"Erm, I don't have any money," I said. "Mom packed me a lunch. She always does." I held up my Batman lunch box. Mom always makes sure I have a healthy lunch. She also makes sure that I won't have extra pocket money to buy desserts. Desserts are for after dinner only, according to her. I am uncertain of her logic but Dad says not to press the issue if I want chocolate cake after dinner.

"Oh no! I'm going to starve! I really wanted to go to the fruit stall, too!" Jimmy said, upset.

I would have offered to share my lunch with Jimmy, but I knew that he didn't like tuna. The last time I offered him a tuna sandwich, he said he wouldn't eat dolphins. It took both Wendy and me to explain to him that dolphins and tuna are two different animals. Plus, dolphins are mammals, not fish! However, Jimmy is still wary and refuses to touch tuna, even the dolphin-safe tuna Mom buys.

"Oh! You could ask Wendy," I said.

"Wendy-is-skinny-so-she-gets-extra-pocket-money-for-lunch," Watson said.

Unfortunately, that is the truth. But all I need is one big growth spurt. Then I could have a cold Milo for lunch. Or a chicken wing. Or French fries. Or a—

"Oh! Okay! She's over where the Primary Five classes are! I'll be right back!" Jimmy said as he dashed off.

By the time Jimmy came back, it was time to head up to class. I looked at him questioningly and he gave me a cheery thumbs-up. I was relieved. The thought of anyone going without food during lunch was horrifying.

Our first period was social studies and Mrs. Lim, our teacher, was already in class. She wrote *WORLD WAR II* on the whiteboard.

"Do you all know what this means?" she asked, pointing to the *II* on the board. A few hands went up, including my own.

"Good, good. For those of you who don't know, this is the Roman numeral for 'two.' These two *I*'s after *World War* mean that this was the second major war that involved almost the entire world," Mrs. Lim said.

She paused to let that sink in.

"Now, did everyone enjoy our visit to Fort Canning yesterday?" Mrs. Lim asked.

There was a variety of responses. Someone mentioned being allergic to grass; someone else said there were mosquitoes; others complained that the vending machines were out of green tea. I wanted to mention that we should have been briefed about the escalator leading up to the park, but before I did, Mrs. Lim interrupted the students.

"I mean, did you all learn anything?" Mrs. Lim said, frowning at everyone. Her brow was crinkled and her lips pressed together. I deduced that if I didn't save the situation soon, we would all end up with extra homework,

and while I usually loved extra homework, I needed to focus on solving the mystery of the ghostly moans tonight.

Bravely, I raised my hand.

"Yes, Samuel?" Mrs. Lim said.

"It's Sherlock, Mrs. Lim!" Jimmy said.

"Be quiet, Jimmy," Mrs. Lim said. But she smiled a bit. Every teacher in school is fond of Jimmy.

"I would like to ask about sally ports, Mrs. Lim," I said.

"Jimmy port!" Jimmy burst in.

"Jimmy, quiet, please. What did I just say?" Mrs. Lim scolded.

"Ahem. As I was saying, I was wondering if you knew about the history of the sally ports at Fort Canning?" I asked.

"I'm impressed that you know what they are called, Samuel. Everybody else kept yelling 'big hole with stairs' yesterday, before running up and down the stairs, even though they had been told not to," Mrs. Lim said. "There used to be quite a few sally ports at Fort Canning, but there's only one left now. The one that's close to Hotel Fort Canning."

That's what Nazhar's dad had told him, too!

"No, I found—" Jimmy burst in again, jumping up in his excitement.

"Jimmy!" Mrs. Lim and I said at the same time. Jimmy pouted and sat back down.

"Did soldiers die in battle in those sally ports?" I asked.

Mrs. Lim looked surprised.

"What a strange question, Samuel. Why do you ask that?" she said.

"I . . . no reason. I was just wondering, as there was a war going on," I replied.

"Is Fort Canning haunted, Mrs. Lim?" one of the boys sitting behind me asked.

"Of course not. Don't talk nonsense!" she replied. "Let's talk about what you all learned from the Battle Box."

"The-vending-machine-there-did-not-appreciate-having-its-buttons-pressed-repeatedly," Watson said.

"Did anyone learn anything at all about the history of Fort Canning?" Mrs. Lim said, sounding exasperated. "Can anyone at least tell me why Fort Canning is called Fort Canning?"

"It was named after Charles John Canning!" Jimmy said.

The entire class fell into a stunned silence.

"That's right, Jimmy," Mrs. Lim said. She looked surprised as well. "Viscount Charles John Canning. How did you know that?"

"Nazhar told me! He knows lots of things about history and war because of his dad," Jimmy said. "He even told me all about the money the Japanese introduced during the Japanese occupation!"

I was really impressed by Nazhar! I made a mental note to ask if he had any books on history I could borrow.

"It's good that you're learning things, Jimmy," Mrs. Lim said. "Anyone else learned anything from our excursion?"

"Why weren't snacks provided for the bus ride back to school, Mrs. Lim?" someone asked.

We were all given extra homework.

◦◦◦

CHAPTER SIX

"Lunchtime! Lunchtime! I'm going to get my snack! See you later!" Jimmy yelled as he scampered off.

I saw Wendy sitting at our usual spot, so I waved at her, and she waved back. As I was walking over to her, Nazhar came up to me suddenly, looking nothing like his usual self.

"Sherlock, I've lost my *duit pisang*!" Nazhar said. "My dad is going to be so upset! They were the only two notes he had! They don't print them anymore!"

"Why did you bring something so valuable to school, Nazhar?" I asked.

"I-am-valuable. Why-do-I-have-to-come-to-school-with-you-every-day?" Watson asked.

"Because Mom said you're a troublemaker and she can't leave you alone at home," I said. Actually, Mom had not said that, but she did say Watson would be lonely without anybody else at home. I didn't want to test her hypothesis out. He was my robot, after all, and I had to take good care of all my friends.

"I brought them to school for my presentation, which is after lunch, but now I've lost my *duit pisang*!" Nazhar said. "And I'm presenting first!"

I immediately switched into detective mode. There was a mystery to be solved! My new friend was in trouble, and I don't like it when any of my friends are upset.

"Okay, when was the last time you remember holding the notes in your hand, Nazhar?" I asked. "It may help if you close your eyes and try to visualize them." I once found my missing glasses this way. I closed my eyes and saw myself sneaking into the kitchen and opening the freezer door to get chocolate ice cream. My glasses fogged up because of the cold, so I took them off. Just then, I heard footsteps and I quickly shut the door, leaving my glasses inside!

"I think . . . I think it was when Dad gave them to me this morning," Nazhar replied, opening his eyes. "And he told me to take good care of them."

"And what did you do with them after that?" I asked.

"That's the problem. I don't remember. I thought I put them in my wallet, but they aren't there. I thought I might have inserted them into my file with the notes for my presentation, but they're not there, either. I can't remember," Nazhar said, frowning.

"Okay, let's retrace your steps," I said. "When was the first time you opened your wallet today?"

"I think . . . I took my wallet out to give money to Eliza for our teacher's birthday gift," Nazhar said.

"Then let's ask Eliza!" I said. I wasn't looking forward to talking to Eliza, but I had to help Nazhar!

Nazhar, Watson, and I ran around looking for Eliza and finally found her at the school bookshop buying a birthday card.

"Hi there!" I said, trying to sound cheerful. "We need your help."

"Do you need me to explain the meaning of *preternatural* to you?" Eliza said, her eyes unkind.

I was going to say, once again, that ghosts did not exist, but time was of the essence! Now was not the time to get into an argument. Anyway, everyone knows that *preternatural* and *supernatural* mean the same thing. One is just a fancier way of saying the other.

"That is not necessary at this juncture. We merely need to find out if you remember Nazhar giving you money for your teacher's birthday present this morning," I said.

"Yes, he did. Why?" Eliza asked suspiciously.

"Is it possible I accidentally paid you with old Japanese money?" Nazhar said.

"With what? I'm pretty sure I would have noticed if you gave me strange money," Eliza said, crossing her arms over her chest. She looked impatient.

"Could you please check, Eliza?" Nazhar asked. "It's important."

Sighing deeply, Eliza pulled a white envelope filled with money from her pocket and sifted through all the bills.

"All Singaporean dollars in here," she said. "Are you missing something? Maybe the ghosts from Fort Canning followed you back home and stole it!"

I couldn't help myself.

"There are no such things as ghosts!" I said.

"It's okay, Sherlock," Nazhar said, somewhat dejected. "Thanks for checking anyway, Eliza."

"Did you go anywhere else between class and lunch?" I asked while we were walking away.

"What if I dropped the notes somewhere and they flew away and I'll never get them back?" Nazhar said worriedly.

"That is a possibility, but let's not focus on the worst-case scenario until we've investigated all other scenarios," I said. "You've got to focus on remembering what else happened this morning."

"Wait! Before school started, I went to the canteen to buy Milo from the drinks stall. That's actually the first time I took my wallet out," Nazhar said.

My stomach grumbled at the mention of Milo. It was lunchtime and I was very hungry, but I had to help my friend!

"Then let's go back to the canteen," I said.

The canteen was super crowded and the line at the drinks stall was very long, so we couldn't ask the drinks-stall auntie any questions just yet. Instead, we found Wendy and sat with her. She had saved us seats.

"What took you guys so long?" Wendy asked. "Lunch is almost over and Jimmy is still in the fruit stall line."

"Did you get your new paintbrush already?" Nazhar said.

"Wait, if you have extra money to buy things, why are you not using it to buy chicken wings or hot dogs?" I asked.

"That-is-why-Wendy-is-tall-and-skinny," Watson said.

I glared at my robot.

"What's wrong, Nazhar?" Wendy asked.

"I've lost my *duit pisang*. How am I going to do my banana money presentation now?" Nazhar said, his hands clenched tight with worry.

Suddenly, everything clicked into place.

"Come with me! I know exactly where your *duit pisang* is!" I said. I led them straight to the long line at the fruit stall, where Jimmy was exactly seven students back.

"Hi, Sherlock! Hi, Watson! Hi, Nazhar! Hi, Wendy! I've been waiting beyond forever! Almost ten minutes!" Jimmy said cheerfully.

"Let me see what's in your hand, Jimmy!" I said. Jimmy held out both hands.

"AH-HA!" I cried.

"My *duit pisang*!" Nazhar said. "Jimmy, why did you take them? I thought I had lost them!"

Jimmy looked worried. "You said I could borrow money . . . ?"

"Oh! I completely forgot about that!" Nazhar said.

"This must be what happened," I said

confidently. "Jimmy forgot to bring money to school for lunch today. When I sent Jimmy to borrow money from Wendy, she said she couldn't lend him any because she needed to buy a paintbrush," I said.

Wendy nodded. She waved her new paintbrush at me happily.

"You must have overheard and, being the nice guy that you are, you lent him money yourself," I continued.

"Yeah, but I had to go to the restroom, so I gave him my wallet," Nazhar said. "But why did you take those two dollars and not a regular two-dollar note?"

"I'm sure Jimmy didn't take them on purpose, right?" Wendy said. Though we argue sometimes, when it is crunch time, Wendy is a big sister, and always protective of little brothers.

"I only borrowed it! I was going to return it tomorrow, remember? You said it was all right!" Jimmy said. He looked worried.

"And you were originally going to take a regular two-dollar note, weren't you, Jimmy?" I said. Jimmy nodded frantically.

"But then he saw your *duit pisang* and decided that since he wanted to eat bananas for lunch, he would take the banana money!" I concluded.

Jimmy nodded even more frantically. "I figured since I wanted bananas, I would leave your regular money so you could buy whatever you wanted."

"But, Jimmy, this money is completely useless," Nazhar said. "Even though it's two bills that say 'One Dollar,' this kind of money was only used during the Japanese occupation."

"Oh! I didn't know that! You said it was *duit pisang*, so I thought I could use it for *pisang*! I was going to give you two dollars back tomorrow! I thought it would be the same! I'm so sorry, Nazhar!" Jimmy said. He was upset.

"How did you know that *duit pisang* was

banana money, Jimmy?" Wendy asked. She was patting him on his shoulder.

"Jimmy is Peranakan, Wendy. He understands some Malay. Right, Jimmy?" I said.

"Yes," Jimmy said, still nodding frantically. "I learned it from Mama!"

"It's okay, Jimmy. I know you didn't do it on purpose. Here's a regular two-dollar note for your bananas," Nazhar said, handing Jimmy a note from his wallet. He grinned at Jimmy.

"Yay! Thanks, Nazhar! You're the best! No, wait, Sherlock's the best! No, wait, Watson's the best! No, wait, Wendy's the best! No, wait, you're all the best!" Jimmy cried. He finally made it to the front of the line and got his two bananas. And as easily as that, I had solved the Case of the Disappearing *Duit Pisang*.

"But-Sherlock-still-does-not-have-pocket-money-to-buy-anything," Watson added. "He-has-to-grow-taller-and-thinner-first."

I really needed to have a talk with my robot.

"By the way, in all the excitement about my banana money, we never talked about what happened last night at Fort Canning," Nazhar said.

"ARRRRRRGGGGGGHHHHHHHHHH!!!!!!" Watson said.

"Watson! Stop!" I said.

The ARRGGHHING-ing once again stopped mid-ARGH.

I quickly told them what had happened last night, rushing through the parts where Dad and I were carried away by Watson.

"Ghosts exist! Ghosts exist!" Jimmy cried. Now that he had his bananas, he could focus on scaring himself.

"There are no such things as ghosts!" I said firmly.

"Then how would you explain the ghostly moans you and your dad heard last night?" Nazhar asked in the calm way that he had.

"There has to be a reasonable explanation for it," I said. "We haven't even had a chance to check the readings from our equipment. Perhaps it was the wind or—"

"It was ghosts!" Jimmy said, flapping his arms about like a chicken.

"For the last time, ghosts don't exist," I said. "You guys come over later and we'll go through all the readings and recordings Dad and I got last night. I will prove once and for all that there are no such things as ghosts!"

◦◦◦

CHAPTER SEVEN

"Let's check the thermometer first!" I said.

Everybody had gotten permission to come over after school, so we all gathered at my house to review the results obtained from the equipment we had taken to Fort Canning Park last night.

"I was carrying it, so I know the readings will be entirely correct," I continued. "The hypothesis is that temperature drops when there is a ghostly presence nearby."

I checked the thermometer for the time we were at Fort Canning the night before. "Okay, according to the readings, when we were near the tombstones, the temperature remained stable. Then we moved to the sally port and—"

I gasped.

"What?" Nazhar asked, taking the thermometer from me. "The temperature dropped five degrees."

"That doesn't mean anything!" I said. "Maybe someone turned on an air conditioner nearby."

"In a park?" Wendy asked. "That's ridiculous."

That's true. It was a ridiculous explanation. How embarrassing. Calm down, Sherlock! Think logically!

"Did you guys know that not only does 12+1 =11+2, but the letters in 'twelve plus one' can be rearranged to give you 'eleven plus two'?" I said, trying to calm my brain down with simple logic.

Silence greeted me. I could see everyone squinting in concentration as they tried to puzzle out what I had said. Everyone except Watson, mainly because robots don't squint. Plus, he had a robot brain. Jimmy was staring blankly, his fingers wiggling in confusion.

"Maybe-you-had-your-warm-hand-on-the-sensor-the-whole-time-and-only-removed-it-at-the-sally-port," Watson said.

"Jimmy port!" Jimmy said.

"No! I'm not that careless during an experiment," I said, irritably, "but I guess it's possible. Certainly more possible than ghosts!"

"Or air conditioners in parks," Wendy said.

"Never mind that. Let's check the digital recorder," I said, eager to prove that ghosts were not real. "Watson, please calibrate this so only background noises can be heard."

"I-always-obey," Watson said, taking the recorder and walking slowly over to my laptop. He slowly opened up a sound-editing program.

"Couldn't you have done that yourself?" Nazhar asked. "And faster?"

"Yeah, I forgot Watson couldn't just plug the recorder into himself," I said. "I need to fix that." And remind him when we're in a hurry.

70

When Watson had finally loaded the sound file into the sound-editing program, he lowered the volume on the foreground sounds, which were mostly our conversations and screams from last night, and turned up the volume on the background sounds.

We couldn't hear anything at the tombstones, but when Watson fast-forwarded to when we were at the sally port, we heard something that sounded like voices! The hairs on the back of my neck stood up!

"Those are ghosts!" Jimmy said.

"They can't be!" I said. "Maybe there was someone nearby. Those could just be people's voices, muffled by something."

"Dad, Watson, and you weren't muffled at all!" Wendy said.

"It does sound like EVP, Sherlock," Nazhar said.

"What's that?" Wendy asked.

"It's short for electronic voice phenomena,"

I said, trying to keep the squeaking out of my voice. That sometimes happened when I was scared.

"Exactly. EVP refers to ghostly voices that can only be heard on recordings," Nazhar said.

"However," I interrupted, "EVP has been proven to not be supernatural in origin! It could just be background noises or voices that sound ghostly on the recording!"

"Did you hear these voices when you were there?" Wendy asked.

"No," I had to admit.

"Then the voices only appear on the recording," Nazhar said.

"They might not be voices!" I said. "I'm not convinced that they are supernatural."

"Okay, let's check the EMF meter then," Nazhar said.

I checked the readings from last night, and they were crazy!

"According to this, there were high

electromagnetic fields all over Fort Canning!" I said.

"Electromagnetic fields are a clear indication of supernatural activity," Nazhar said. "Every ghost hunter knows that."

"That's it then!" Wendy said. "We have proven that there are ghosts in Fort Canning!"

"There-is-actually-a-simple-explanation-for-this," Watson said. However, before he could continue, he was interrupted by hysterics from everyone else.

"Yeah! Ghosts!" Jimmy shouted.

"What kind do you think they are?" Wendy asked.

"They could be *hantu galah* or *jenglot*," Nazhar said thoughtfully. "Or even *orang minyak*."

"But then they would have found oil," Jimmy said.

"You're right," Nazhar said. "Maybe they're *jembalang tanah*. Don't mess with those, Sherlock."

Snatch!

"They could be *shuǐ guǐ* or *yuān guǐ*," Wendy said. "Or maybe *è guǐ*!"

"They can't be *è guǐ*," Jimmy said. "We're nowhere near the Hungry Ghost Month! Maybe they're just *guǐ pó*. Mama says those are friendly ghosts."

"It's not any of those," I said. "Ghosts aren't real!"

"Sherlock, you're a man of science," Nazhar said, sounding logical and calm. "Look at the evidence in front of you."

He was right. The readings and recordings were hard to explain, but ghosts weren't real!

Were they?

∘∘∘

CHAPTER EIGHT

KA-BOOM!

"Sam! Don't forget that it's your turn to do the dishes!" Mom called out, her voice more shocking than the crashing thunder.

I was lying snugly under the covers in my bedroom, reading up on debunking supernatural occurrences. A storm raged outside and Mom was nagging at me from the living room.

"Watson—" I said.

"I-did-the-dishes-yesterday. It-is-your-turn-today," Watson replied.

"Fine," I huffed, tossing my comfortable covers away. "You still have to come with me so I can recite my case notes to you."

"Thus-far-I-have-recorded-an-impressive-collection-of-shrieks-and-screams-for-your-case-notes," Watson replied.

The minute I left the safety of my room,

my ears were assailed by a horrendous noise coming from what sounded like a wind instrument.

"**DOO**-doo-doo-doo-**DOO**-doo. **DOO**-doo-doo-doo-**DOO**-doo. **DOO**-doo-doo-doo-**DOO**-doo."

"What horrible tortures are you inflicting on that poor instrument?" I asked, hands clasped over my ears. I stood in front of my sister *doo-doo-doo*-ing away on her recorder. Wendy glared at me but continued puffing away determinedly.

"Your sister is practicing for her music class test, Sam. Leave her alone," Mom replied.

Dad, who was wearing a huge pair of headphones attached to his laptop, grinned at me as I walked by. Like I have always said: Dad is a very smart man.

As I stood on the stool in front of the sink, up to my arms in warm, soapy suds, I started to recount all the facts of the case to Watson.

"Both times we heard it, we were close to the newly discovered sally port," I said.

"The first time, a rock flew out from the sally port," I continued. "Watson, recite what we know about poltergeists."

"They-are-noisy-and-destructive-entities," Watson said.

"**DOO-doo-doo-doo-DOO-doo.**"

"Like Wendy. She's noisily destroying my eardrums," I said.

"They-often-throw-or-hurl-objects-at-their-targets," Watson continued.

"**DOO-doo-doo-doo-DOO-doo.**"

"I'd like to throw something at one specific target," I replied.

"They-seem-to-haunt-specific-locations," Watson said.

"**DOO-doo-doo-doo-DOO-doo.**"

"If only we could get Wendy to move—wait a minute!" I said. Dropping the soapy sponge, I ran into the living room.

"Play it again! Play it again!" I shouted at Wendy, frantically miming her playing the recorder.

"What's the matter, Sam?" Dad asked, removing his headphones.

"I need Wendy to play her recorder exactly like she has been playing it the entire night!" I said. "Watson, I need you to record it!"

"Really, Sam? I was just going to tell Wendy to take a break so that I could watch Discovery Channel," Dad said, looking slightly confused.

"Trust me, Dad! Play it again, Wendy! The one section you've been playing all night!"

"**DOO**-doo-doo-doo-**DOO**-doo. **DOO**-doo-doo-doo-**DOO**-doo. **DOO**-doo-doo-doo-**DOO**-doo."

"Did you get it, Watson?" I asked.

Watson replied: "**DOO**-doo-doo-doo-**DOO**-doo. **DOO**-doo-doo-doo-**DOO**-doo. **DOO**-doo-doo-doo-**DOO**-doo."

"Wow, do I really sound that bad?" Wendy asked.

"Play it again, Watson!" I said.

"**DOO**-doo-doo-doo-**DOO**-doo. **DOO**-doo-doo-doo-**DOO**-doo. **DOO**-doo-doo-doo-**DOO**-doo."

"Wendy! That's enough!" Mom called out. "I mean, that's enough practice, dear."

"That wasn't me!" Wendy shouted back.

Dad was wincing.

"Okay, Watson, now play the ghostly moan!" I said.

"**OOOoooOOOooo. OOOoooOOOooo. OOOoooOOOooo.**"

"Don't you guys get it?" I asked.

Everyone looked at me blankly.

I had solved the Case of the Ghostly Moans in Fort Canning! Now to prove to everyone that ghosts didn't exist!

But I had to wait until the following day. It was raining so heavily that Mom was worried we would all get wet and fall sick. Plus, Watson might rust.

KA-BOOM!

ooo

CHAPTER NINE

After school on Friday, Dad took Wendy, Nazhar, Jimmy, Watson, and me to the Sakae Sushi at Park Mall for dinner. We had delicious sushi and *chawanmushi*. Dad let me have three bowls of the delicious egg custard and made me promise not to tell Mom.

After dinner, we trooped over to Fort Canning and headed for the hidden sally port ("Jimmy port!" Jimmy corrected every chance he got). Everybody seemed tense, but I knew I would put their fears to rest soon. We hid near the 9-Pound Cannon at the top of the Spice Garden path, and waited for the remaining parkgoers to leave. My plan required that the area be free of all bystanders so that they wouldn't interfere.

"My toe itches," Jimmy said. Watson extended one of his arms and tried to scratch it.

"Hee hee hee, stop! That tickles!" Jimmy said, laughing.

"Shhhh!" Wendy tried to stifle Jimmy's laughter.

I poked my head out to make sure nobody had heard us. There didn't seem to be anybody around anymore.

"It looks like we're clear, everybody," I said. "Remember now, we have to go very quietly."

"Ghosts can hear you regardless of how quiet you are," Nazhar said. "They don't hear with ears."

"Because they don't have any!" Jimmy said triumphantly. Then he looked confused. "Wait, how do they hear anything at all without ears?"

"Luckily for us, there are no ghosts, and I'm going to prove it," I said.

I led them out from behind the cannon and we tiptoed straight to the sally port ("Jimmy port!").

We reached the entrance of the sally port before the ghostly moans started up.

"**OOOₒₒₒOOOₒₒₒ. OOOₒₒₒOOOₒₒₒ. OOOₒₒₒOOOₒₒₒ.**"

Everybody tensed up, except Watson and me. When Dad saw me looking at him, he tried to smile. Jimmy's eyes were wide with fear, but I motioned for him to calm down.

"It's not a ghost," I said. "Trust me."

Once the moaning stopped, we continued forward. The tunnel leading from the sally port ("Jimmy port!") was long and winding. We took at least three left turns and four rights, and we were definitely going downward as well.

Periodically, we would hear the ghostly moaning, but it was coming from behind us now.

"That's odd," Nazhar said. "It's not following us. It sounds like it's still at the entrance."

"Perhaps it's only a guardian spirit?" Wendy said.

"And not a very powerful one, since we've clearly breached the entrance," Dad said. "If there were such things as ghosts. Which there are not," Dad continued, sheepishly.

I pointed out the electric cables running on the ceiling of the tunnel to Watson. He nodded.

The end of the tunnel opened into a large bunker. There were wooden beams running from floor to ceiling throughout and a few tables here and there. There was an exit leading to another tunnel across from us. We could hear someone or something rummaging in a corner, but couldn't see what was causing it, though I was pretty sure I knew what it was.

"Okay, Watson," I said, "play it now."

"**DOO**-doo-doo-doo-**DOO**-doo. **DOO**-doo-doo-doo-**DOO**-doo. **DOO**-doo-doo-doo-**DOO**-doo."

"No! That's the wrong one! You should have played the moans!" I whispered.

As it turned out, it didn't really matter. The sound startled the three men in the bunker, and they ran toward the other exit, knocking over a few tables in their haste to escape. One man was dragging a trolley bag behind him as he ran. The wheels on the bag made a really loud rattling sound as they were being pulled over uneven ground!

"Poultry-guests! Poultry-guests!" Jimmy shouted. He started running back the way we had come, arms flapping like a chicken, but then he saw a spider and ran back into the bunker. Watson extended his arms and caught him before he could get too far.

"That went exactly as planned!" I said. "Except for Watson's small hiccup."

"The-plan-was-to-play-the-awful-sound," Watson said. "How-could-I-have-known-you-did-not-mean-that-one?"

"Good job, son!" Dad beamed.

"Wait, what just happened?" Wendy asked. "Those weren't ghosts! They were people!"

"Yeah, ghosts don't scare so easy," Nazhar said. "But who were they?"

"Thieves and crooks," a deep voice said.

We all looked toward the voice and saw a few policemen hauling the three men back into the bunker. The one in charge was an Indian man.

"Now, what are you kids doing here?" he asked.

ooo

CHAPTER TEN

The policemen sat the three men down on the floor while the one in charge walked over to us.

"I'm Officer Siva," he said.

"I'm Sherlock Sam," I said, sticking my hand out. We shook hands.

"So what exactly are you doing here?" Officer Siva asked.

"I was here solving a mystery, sir," I said. "There were ghostly moans coming out of

here that I knew couldn't be from ghosts, since ghosts don't exist."

"He's Singapore's Great—" Jimmy started.

"Not yet, Jimmy," Wendy said. "He hasn't explained anything to us yet."

"Yeah," Nazhar said. "What about all the proof of ghosts?"

"It's like I told you from the start," I said. "Ghosts aren't real."

"Then explain the digital recorder," Jimmy said. "The recording clearly had ghostly voices in the background!"

"But those weren't ghostly voices," I said. "The digital recorder is very sensitive. It actually caught the voices of these three gentlemen, but because they were so far away from where we recorded, the recording sounded faint and garbled."

"Plus-the-voices-bounced-off-the-tunnel-walls-disguising-their-voices-even-further," Watson said.

"What about the thermometer?" Wendy asked. "The reading clearly showed a drop in temperature when you got to the sally port."

"Jimmy port!" Jimmy said.

"Can't you feel the temperature?" I asked. "It's like I said before: air conditioners in the park. It's just that they were in this bunker and we couldn't see them." I pointed to the four air-conditioning units in the bunker.

"But the cool air escaped out of the entrance," Nazhar said.

"Exactly," I said.

"But what about the EMF meter?" Nazhar asked. "It went crazy, remember? That's a clear indication of paranormal activity."

"That was actually the easiest thing to figure out," I said. "But you guys scared me so badly last night, I'm ashamed to admit I couldn't think clearly. Watson, show them."

Watson pulled out the EMF meter from his secret compartment and turned it on. It immediately registered an enormous spike in electromagnetism.

"As-I-tried-to-tell-you-last-night-I-am-causing-these-readings," Watson said. "I-am-a-robot-with-a-magnetic-personality."

"Always make sure you have a control group during an experiment to compare against," I

said. "Otherwise, you could totally misread your findings."

"And the ghostly moans?" Dad asked.

"Wendy helped me figure that out, actually," I said.

"I did?" she asked.

"Last night, when you were playing your recorder, you were playing the same refrain over and over," I said. "It made me realize that the ghostly moans were also the same refrain, over and over."

I walked over to a stereo in the corner, removed the audio equipment attached to it, and pressed play.

"**OOO**oo**OOO**ooo. **OOO**oo**OOO**ooo. **OOO**oo**OOO**ooo."

"It's on a loop," I said. "The ghostly moan has the same duration and changes in pitch every time, and it was piped to the entrance using this audio equipment. They used it to keep people away, in case anybody found the sally port. Like Jimmy did."

"So one of these men threw that rock the first time we heard the moans?" Nazhar asked.

"Yes," I said. "I think they had just entered, or were about to leave, and they wanted us to go away as soon as possible, so they threw the rock to scare us further."

"You are a very clever little boy," Officer Siva said.

"What were these men doing, sir?" Nazhar asked.

"They were making copies of movies and music illegally, and selling them all over Singapore," Officer Siva said. "That's a very big offense, and even bigger when you take into account the size of their operation."

"There is one thing I can't figure out though, Officer Siva," I said.

"Something Sherlock Sam can't figure out? Impossible!" Officer Siva said, smiling.

"Why are the police here? We didn't even

know a crime was being committed," I said. "I figured out that it was a man-made sound, and it's logical that it would be used to hide something, but I didn't call the police!"

"Well, just two nights ago, quite a few hotel guests from Hotel Fort Canning complained that they heard really loud screaming. It sounded like people were being tortured. The hotel called the police. We didn't find anything, but just to be safe, my men and I decided to come back to monitor the situation," Officer Siva replied. "We came over to investigate once we heard the commotion."

"Screaming?" Nazhar asked. "But that wasn't the sound the criminals were playing. That was a moan."

"ARRRRRRGGGGGGHHHHHHHHH!!!!!!" Watson said.

"Watson! Enough!" I said.

The ARRGGHHING-ing once again stopped mid-ARGH.

Dad and I looked at each other in horror. The hotel guests had heard our screaming!

"Well, at least we helped catch the criminals?" Dad said finally.

Wendy snickered a little but she was still smiling at Dad and me.

"One of the criminals had illegal copies of

the music and movies in his trolley bag, didn't he?" I said. "I noticed the bag was unzipped as he was running away. The contents must have spilled out. That's why you were able to arrest him and his accomplices on the spot."

"You're really a very clever boy, Sherlock," Officer Siva said. "You got it exactly right. He left a trail of illegal DVDs behind him as he ran!"

"And we would have gotten away with it if it wasn't for you *kaypoh* kids!" one of the arrested men shouted.

"It's true," Officer Siva said. "We would never have caught them without you and your clever brain."

"Now?" Jimmy asked, looking hopeful.

"Fine," Wendy said.

"He's Singapore's Greatest Kid Detective!" Jimmy shouted.

"Only-when-he-does-not-run-away-screaming," Watson replied.

*   *   *

A few days later, Dad came to my room with a letter.

"Guess what Neil deGrasse Tyson has to say about ghosts, Dad," I said.

"What?" he asked.

"'If each dead person became a ghost, there'd be more than 100 billion ghosts haunting us all,'" I said.

"Creepy," Dad said. "But kind of cool."

"That-is-what-Dr.-Tyson-said-as-well," Watson said.

Dad beamed. He liked being compared to Neil deGrasse Tyson.

"What's that in your hand, Dad?" I asked.

"Oh, right, I almost forgot," he said. "It's for you."

"Really?" I said excitedly. "I never get mail!"

I noticed it was from Officer Siva and tore it open quickly.

I read it aloud:

Dear Sherlock Sam,

Thank you very much for your invaluable assistance in bringing the DVD bootleggers to justice. We would never have known about them if not for you. You are an extremely bright boy, and I think your friend Jimmy is right when he says you are Singapore's Greatest Kid Detective.

I am sure we will see each other again very soon. In fact, if your parents don't mind, I may call on you for help sooner rather than later.

Keep studying, and keep solving mysteries.

Your friend,

Officer Siva

"Wow," I said when I finished reading. "Do you really think I could help him with cases?"

"We'll have to clear it with Mom, but I don't see why not," Dad said.

I looked at the letter again. "I'm going to keep this forever," I said.

"Actually, Sam," Dad said, "is it okay if I frame it and put it in the living room?"

"Dad," I said, "that would be awesome."

THE END

GLOSSARY

Animatronics—Mechanical creations designed to look alive.

Arthur Conan Doyle, Sir—The celebrated author of the original Sherlock Holmes stories and novels.

Battle Box, the—The underground bunker beneath Fort Canning that was used by the British as an emergency bomb-proof command center during the Malayan campaign and the Battle of Singapore during World War II. It is now a museum and tourist attraction.

Chawanmushi—A Japanese egg custard usually served in a teacup-like bowl. The custard is flavored with soy sauce, dashi, and mirin, and contains various ingredients, such as shiitake mushrooms and shrimp.

Duit Pisang—Malay for "banana money," this Japanese-issued currency was used in Japanese-occupied territories in Southeast Asia during World War II.

È Guǐ—A chubby ghost that supposedly appears during Hungry Ghost Month and searches for food. It has a very small mouth and suffers from insatiable hunger.

Electromagnetic Field—A measurable field produced by moving electrically charged objects, like balloons that have been rubbed on your head, which affect all charged objects near them. It is one of the four fundamental forces of nature.

Electromagnetic Field Meter—A scientific instrument that measures electromagnetic fields and their changes over time.

Electronic Voice Phenomena (EVP)—Electronically generated noises that sound like ghostly speech, but are not supernatural in the slightest. EVP are instead static, stray radio transmissions and background noises that sound like voices.

Guǐ Pó—A ghost that supposedly takes the form of a kind and friendly old woman, usually a domestic servant of a rich family who returns to help the family with housekeeping and childcare.

Hantu Galah—A very tall and thin ghost found among trees and bamboo. To defeat it, one picks up a stick and breaks it.

Hungry Ghost Month—During this traditional Chinese festival, celebrated during the seventh month of the lunar calendar, it is believed that ghosts, including those of deceased ancestors, visit the living. Offerings of food are made, and joss paper is burned for the benefit of the ghosts.

Jembalang Tanah—An earth demon that supposedly resembles a goblin and is thought to be very dangerous if not properly appeased.

Jenglot—A mythological vampire found in Malaysian and Indonesian folklore. It looks like a tiny living doll.

Kaypoh—Nosy or meddling. A busybody.

Lemak—Malay for "rich and creamy."

Lemongrass—Widely used in Asian cuisine, this herb has a citrus flavor and is used in teas, soups, and curries.

Mama—Grandmother.

Milo—A chocolate malt drink that is popular with kids in Singapore.

Nasi Lemak—A Malay dish of rice cooked with coconut milk and pandan leaf, commonly served with cucumber slices, dried anchovies, roasted peanuts, a hard-boiled egg, and chili paste.

Neil deGrasse Tyson, Dr.—An astrophysicist and science communicator, Dr. Tyson is currently the director of the Hayden Planetarium at the American Museum of Natural History in New York City. He is a fierce proponent of "science literacy."

Orang Minyak—Malay for "oily man," this spirit is believed to reside near bodies of water and goes after women almost exclusively.

Pandan—A tropical plant with leaves that are often used as flavoring in Southeast Asia cooking.

P4—Short form for Primary Four.

Peranakan—Straits Chinese. Descendants of Chinese settlers who settled in Malacca, Penang, and Singapore. Peranakan culture is a hybrid culture incorporating Chinese and Malay influences.

Poltergeist—An invisible but disruptive ghost that throws objects and makes noises, such as knocking. Occasionally, a poltergeist will pinch the living.

Primary Four—Fourth grade.

Rochor Original Beancurd—Arguably the most famous bean curd stall in Singapore. Celebrities such as chef Anthony Bourdain, actress Michelle Yeoh, and photographer Russel Wong have tried the bean curd sold at this stall.

Sally Port—Small, secret doors that lead in and out of military forts. They help people enter and leave undetected. Fort Canning has three known sally ports. The "Jimmy port" in this story is fictitious.

Shuǐ Guǐ—Chinese for "water ghost," this is supposedly the spirit of someone who has drowned.

Supper—A late-night meal, taken around 11:00 p.m. in Singapore.

Tau Huay—A dessert made with very soft bean curd served in a clear sweet syrup.

Upper Primary—Fourth, fifth, and sixth grades.

World War II—Also known as the Second World War (1939–1945), this was a global war that involved a majority of the world's nations, which were split into two opposing factions: the Allies and the Axis powers. Japan, an Axis power, occupied Southeast Asia, including Singapore, during World War II, from 1941 to 1945.

You Char Kway—A long strip of dough that is deep-fried until golden brown. It is usually eaten for breakfast or supper, as an accompaniment to congee, soy milk, or tau huay.

Yuān Guǐ—This is supposedly the spirit of someone who has died a wrongful death and roams the world seeking justice.

Zombies—Reanimated corpses that supposedly like eating brains. The U.S. Centers for Disease Control and Prevention has a zombie preparedness website (*www.cdc.gov/phpr/zombies.htm*), but it is really to help you prepare for possible real-life emergencies, as zombies are not real.

ABOUT THE CHARACTERS

SAMUEL TAN CHER LOCK a.k.a. SHERLOCK SAM

A ten-year-old boy with eyes bigger than his tummy. Sherlock's heroes are Sherlock Holmes, Batman, and his dad. Extremely smart and observant, Sherlock often takes it upon himself to solve any and all mysteries—big or small. He loves comics and superheroes!

WATSON

Built by Sherlock to be his trusty, cheery sidekick, Watson is, instead, a "grumpy old man" who is reluctantly drawn into Sherlock's adventures, or, as Watson perceives them, his misadventures. Watson is environmentally friendly.

WENDY

Sherlock's older sister. A year older than Sherlock, Wendy is a very talented artist, but she is terrible at Chinese. Sherlock would like to be taller than her one day soon. She doesn't like wearing dresses or skirts.

JIMMY

Sherlock's classmate Jimmy is the only boy in a Peranakan family with four sisters. He seems much younger than his actual age, because everything is exciting and magical to Jimmy. He has terrible handwriting.

DAD

An engineer, Sherlock's dad is a scientific genius, but is rather forgetful and bumbling in real life. He has never stopped reading superhero comics—a love he's passed on to his son.

MOM

A homemaker, Sherlock's mom is half-Peranakan and is constantly experimenting in the kitchen. Sherlock often wonders why she tempts him with food, then does not allow him to eat his fill.

NAZHAR

Nazhar is the big brother of the group. Usually shy and quiet, Nazhar will stand up for his friends when they are threatened. Sherlock admires him for his knowledge of history, which Nazhar picked up from his dad.

ELIZA

One of the prettiest and most popular girls in school, Eliza often bullies kids she sees as weird or geeky—for example, Sherlock Sam and his friends. Eliza spends a lot of time in front of the bathroom mirror, making sure her hair is neat.

OFFICER SIVA

A deputy superintendent in the Singapore Police Force, Officer Siva is an experienced policeman who is extremely impressed by the intelligence he sees in Sherlock Sam. He loves kaya toast and coffee from Chin Mee Chin, a bakery in Katong.

ABOUT THE AUTHORS

The writers behind the pseudonym A. J. Low are the husband-and-wife team of Adan Jimenez and Felicia Low-Jimenez. Born in California to Mexican immigrant parents, Adan became an immigrant himself when he moved to Singapore after graduating from New York University with an English literature degree. He previously cowrote a children's book, *Twisted Journeys #22: Hero City*. He loves comics, LEGO, books, movies, games (analog and video), *Doctor Who*, and sandwiches, and one day hopes to own a store that sells all these things. Felicia was born and raised in Singapore. She spent most of her childhood with her head in the clouds and her nose buried in a book, and now daydreams of owning her own bookstore. She has a graduate degree in literary theory and the *Sherlock Sam* series is Felicia's debut writing effort, after accumulating years of experience buying, selling, and marketing books.

You can contact the authors at *sherlock.sam.sg@gmail.com* or by visiting *sherlocksam.wordpress.com* and *facebook.com/SherlockSamSeries*.

ABOUT THE ILLUSTRATOR

Andrew Tan (also known as drewscape) is a full-time freelance illustrator and an Eisner-nominated comic artist. He illustrates for print ads and magazines, and also enjoys storyboarding and illustrating for picture-book projects. During his free time, he creates his own comics for the fun of it. In his home studio, you'll find an overflow of art tools of all kinds as he loves experimenting with them. He already has too many fountain pens and tells himself that he will stop buying more. Andrew published his first graphic novel, *Monsters, Miracles & Mayonnaise*, in 2012.

LOOK OUT FOR SHERLOCK SAM'S NEXT ADVENTURE!

Get ready for Sherlock Sam's next adventure, this time, in an international school in Singapore!

In *Sherlock Sam and the Sinister Letters in Bras Basah*, Sherlock Sam is all set to discover what an international school is really like, but one of the students is receiving strange letters that are causing grave concern. Can Singapore's Greatest Kid Detective use his super intelligence to help his new friend?